For Jean

William Collins Sons & Co Ltd
London · Glasgow · Sydney · Auckland
Toronto · Johannesburg

First published 1989
© text Mike Ratnett 1989
© illustrations June Goulding 1989

ISBN 0 00 191135 X

A CIP Catalogue record for this book
is available from the British Library

Printed and bound in Belgium by
Proost International Book Production

TOGG
and
LEFTOVER

Mike Ratnett and June Goulding

COLLINS

Togg was a caveman. He lived all alone in his cave, deep in a valley.

One morning Togg was clearing out the back of his cave
when he found a huge egg.

"This will make a wonderful breakfast," he thought. "I will invite all my friends to share it."
He rolled the egg outside into the warm sunshine, and set off over the hills to find everyone.

The day grew hotter and hotter. As the sun beat down on the egg, weird things began to happen. There was a strange tapping sound and the huge egg wobbled and shook. Then, "Craaaack!" the shell split open.

When Togg and his friends returned, all that was left of the enormous egg were huge, broken pieces of shell.

"We're too late," said Flowulf.
"Somebody must have eaten it," mumbled Coppertop.
"Fancy leaving it lying around like that," said Redbeard.
And they turned right round and set off home again, feeling very disappointed and hungry.

Togg was so upset about his egg he went straight to bed and stayed there for the rest of the day.
"I wonder what happened to it?" he thought.

Togg's friends had not gone very far, when suddenly an enormous monster leapt out at them.

"Boo!" it shouted.
"Help!" shrieked the cave people, and they ran to hide.

Everything went quiet.
"It's gone," whispered Redbeard and they all crept out.
But the huge monster was waiting.

"Blaaah!" it went, jumping at them again.
Togg's friends fled home as fast as they could.

The next day, Togg woke up feeling very hungry.
I must go out hunting, he thought. And he went off to see if his
friends would come too.

Togg's friends were at Redbeard's cave.
"We've seen a monster," said Coppertop. "It's gigantic!"
"I wonder where it came from?" thought Togg. And then he remembered his egg.

"I must find the monster," thought Togg.
So he set out to look for it.

He looked to the left…

He looked to the right...

He looked up high...

He looked down low...

but he could not see a monster anywhere.

By now Togg was very tired, so he lay down
under a tree for a rest.
"Boo!" shouted someone, and
Togg woke with a start.
It was the monster.

Togg jumped up and ran for his life. The huge creature chased after him.

They ran and ran and ran...

Togg ran until he could go no further.
The monster came closer and closer.

He opened his mouth and…licked Togg on the chin.
"Why, you only want to be friends!" Togg laughed.

The creature was so pleased to see Togg laugh that he laughed too. Then he flipped Togg onto his back and gave him a ride home.

Once the cave people saw that the creature was friendly, they all came out to meet him.
"You look like a dinosaur," said one of them, "left over from long ago."

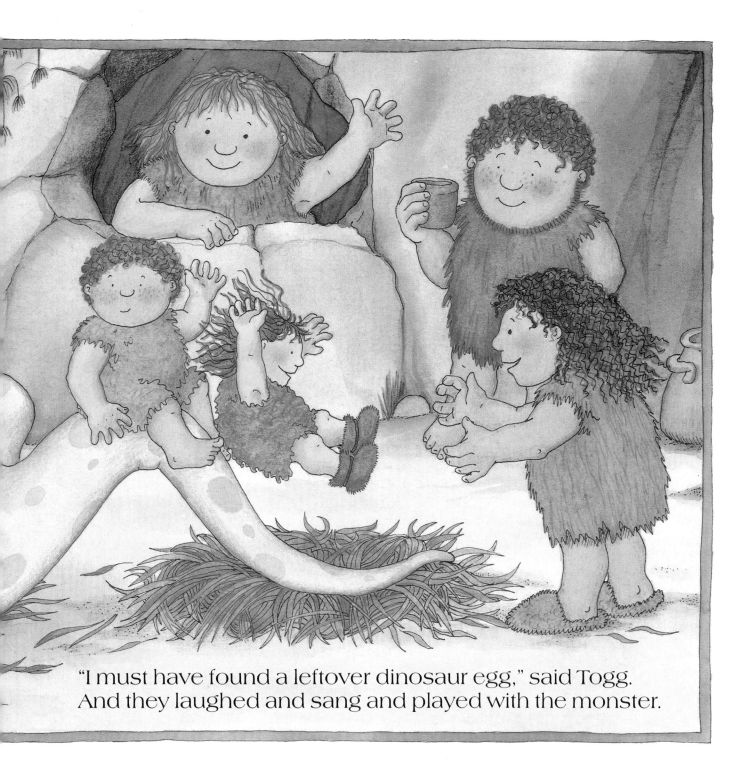

"I must have found a leftover dinosaur egg," said Togg.
And they laughed and sang and played with the monster.

And from that day on the dinosaur was Togg's friend and went to live with him in his cave. Togg called him "Leftover" because that is exactly what he was.